It's not dangerous!

It's OK to be scared, but you've got this!

About the Author:

Dr. Daniela Owen is a psychologist in the SF Bay Area who brings to life healthy mind concepts and strategies for children everywhere.
For more about the author please check out
drdanielaowen.com

For Lila Skye and Milo Grant

For all inquiries, please contact us at:
info@puppysmiles.org

To see more of our books, visit us at:
www.PuppyDogsAndIceCream.com

You can do it!

You can handle it!

This book is given with love...

_____

_____

Sometimes, things can feel

really scary...

These may be things that other kids find scary too.

...Or they may be things that most kids don't find scary at all.

When the things we find scary
are not actually dangerous,
then it's time to be brave!

It's not dangerous!
It's OK to be scared, but you've got this!
You can do it!
You can handle it!

Being brave is about
facing something that is
scary or hard for you to deal with.

Sometimes we choose to be brave
because it's the right thing to do.

Firefighters, astronauts,
and soldiers are all brave,
and their jobs are really hard!

When something feels scary, our brains may tell us to run away, go and hide, or stay away no matter what.

But we don't always have to listen to what our brains tell us.

Sometimes our brains
play tricks on us and
tell us something is scarier
than it actually is.

Think back, have you ever
been worried, nervous, or
scared to do something new?

Then once you did it,
you were so glad you did?

Being brave is tough!
It's tough for firefighters,
astronauts, and soldiers.

It can be tough for kids too,
but you can do it.

BRAVE PATH
You are brave!
Go for it!
Be courageous!
You've got this!

One way to be brave is
to talk to yourself
in an encouraging way.
When your brain is saying,
not so fast...
tell yourself, "I can handle it!"

Then you will feel much more
confident and brave.

How about you give it a try?

"I can do this!"

"I am Brave."

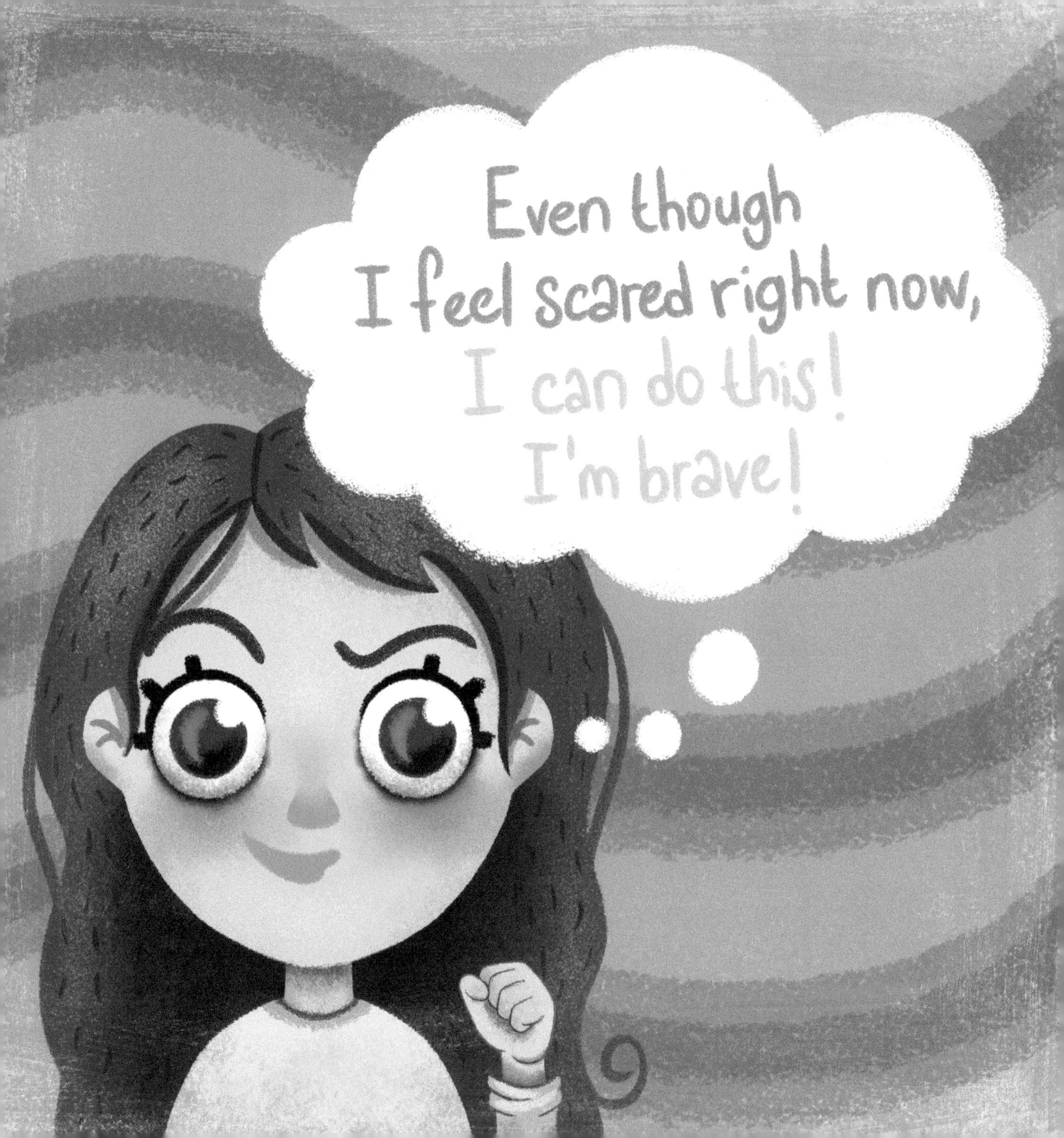
Even though
I feel scared right now,
I can do this!
I'm brave!

Cheering ourselves on is one of the best ways to help us be brave.

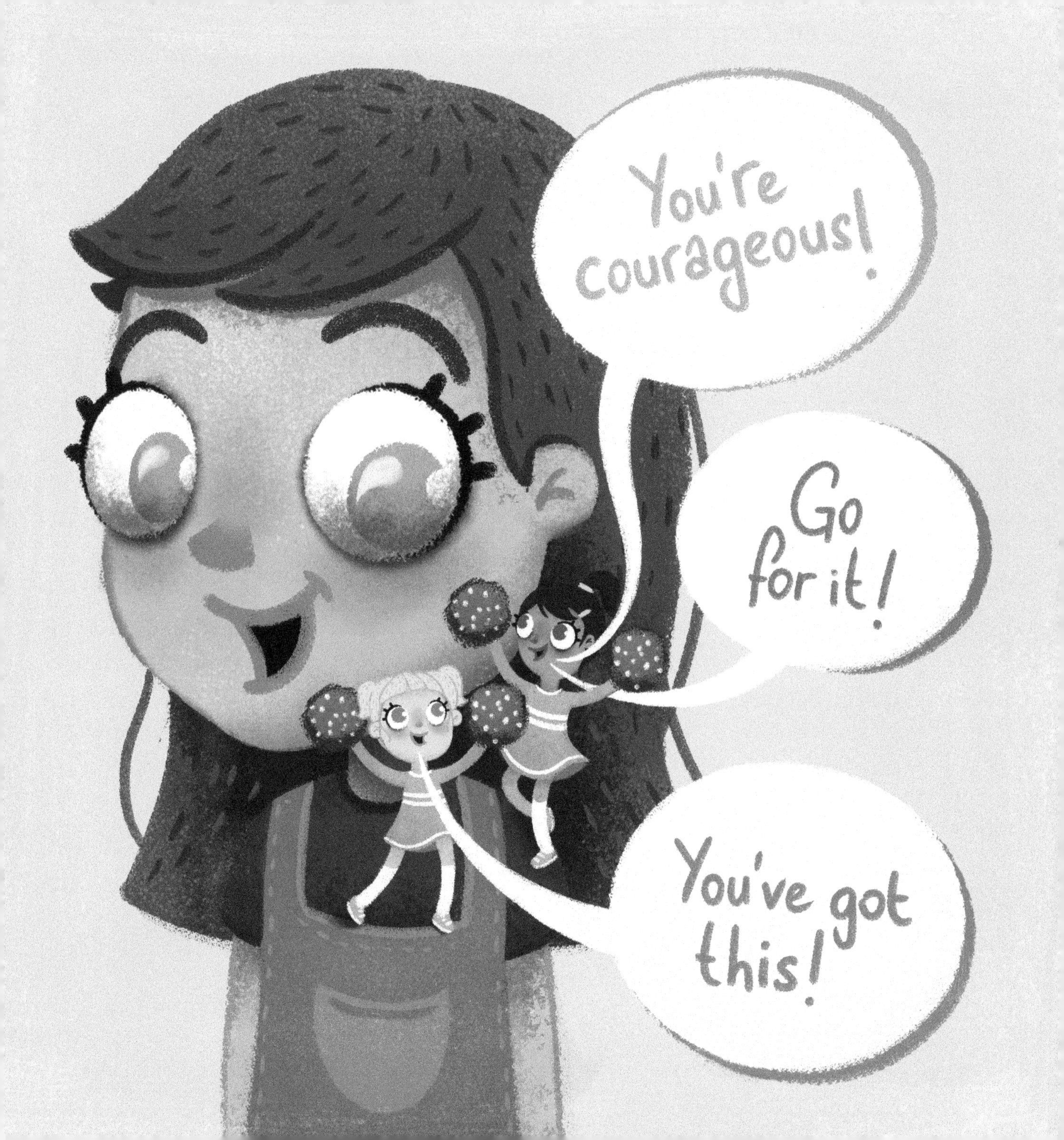
You're courageous!
Go for it!
You've got this!

Another way to help ourselves feel brave is by making a plan to do something brave.

When we set a goal and make a promise to ourselves, we are more likely to achieve our goal.

When the time comes
to do the brave thing, remember:

"I made a promise to myself,
and I will be very glad that
I kept my promise!"

What helps the most
is doing something brave
and discovering that
you can handle it.

Once we do something brave,
we are always glad we did.

We feel extremely proud of ourselves
which makes it a tiny bit easier
to be brave the next time.

A great thing to do
after we have been brave
is to reward ourselves.

Being brave is tough and
when we accomplish tough things,
it's nice to give ourselves a reward.

We can reward ourselves
with a pat on the back,
a self-hug, or by telling ourselves
how great it is that
we chose to be brave.

Remind yourself...

Right Now, I am Brave!

CPSIA information can be obtained
at www.ICGtesting.com
Printed in the USA
BVHW061631170321
602780BV00003B/38